The Case of Hermie
the Missing Hamster

by James Preller
illustrated by R. W. Alley

A
LITTLE APPLE
PAPERBACK

SCHOLASTIC INC.
New York Toronto London Auckland Sydney

For
Lisa

ISBN 0-590-69125-2

Text copyright © 1998 by James Preller. Illustrations copyright © 1998 by R. W. Alley. All rights reserved. Published by Scholastic Inc. LITTLE APPLE PAPERBACKS, SCHOLASTIC and logos are trademarks and/or registered trademarks of Scholastic Inc.

12 11 10 9 8 7 6 5 4   8 9/9 0 1 2 3/0

Printed in the U.S.A.   40
First Scholastic printing, September 1998

CONTENTS

Chapter One
Jigsaw Jones, Private Eye

It was Sunday afternoon, 4:36 P.M. I was in my office on the dirty side of town. Okay, actually I was in my tree house in the backyard. But it had a wooden sign that read OFFICE.

And it *was* dirty. But that's no big deal. When you're in my line of work, you get used to a little dirt.

No, I don't make mud cakes for a living. I'm a detective. For a dollar a day, I make problems go away.

I was working on my new "Life in the

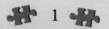 1

Jurassic" jigsaw puzzle. It wasn't going great. Okay, it was going crummy. My dog, Rags, yapped below. I told him to be quiet. Rags kept on barking. It was one of those days.

Suddenly a voice called out, "Hey, Jigsaw, you up there?" My next-door neighbor, Wingnut O'Brien, climbed the tree house ladder. His real name was Timothy, but everyone called him Wingnut because of his ears. They were three sizes too big for his head.

Wingnut didn't mind his nickname. In fact, he liked it. Wingnut was proud of his oversize ears. They made him feel special. Go figure. I thought they made him look . . . well . . . like a wing nut.

"What are you up to?" Wingnut asked.

"Oh, about ten feet," I answered.

Wingnut looked down. "Uh, yeah," he said.

Wingnut was six years old, a year

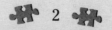

younger than me. He wore blue jeans, a hockey jersey, and a frown.

"Listen, Jigsaw, I've got a problem," Wingnut said.

"I make problems go away," I answered. "But it'll cost you. You know my rate: I get a dollar a day."

Wingnut's eyes started to water. Oh, brother. I handed him a box of Kleenex. In this line of work, you see a lot of tears. It pays to keep Kleenex around — especially if you don't have the stomach to watch somebody slobber all over his new hockey jersey.

Wingnut looked at me with sad, pitiful eyes. Between sobs and sighs, he sputtered, "Hermie's gone."

Hermie was Wingnut's golden hamster. It looked like this might be a job for Jigsaw Jones. Business had been slow and I needed the cash. Puzzles don't grow on trees, you know.

See, I've been solving problems in my neighborhood — and at school — ever since kindergarten. I was in second grade now, in Ms. Gleason's class. But some things never change. There are always problems — missing cupcakes, stolen baseball mitts, lost hamsters.

There will always be a need for me: Jigsaw Jones, Private Eye.

Chapter Two
A Slithery Suspect

I nodded toward an empty glass jar. Wingnut dug into his pockets. He dropped in two quarters, two dimes, a rubber band, and five nickels.

"You're a nickel short," I pointed out.

Wingnut's face got all squinched up. Like he was going to cry or something. "You can owe me," I said.

I took out my detective journal. It was a big, fat notebook. I never left home without it. I turned to a clean page and wrote the following words:

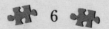

Underneath, I made two neat rows. On the top of one, I wrote Suspects. On the other, Clues. I underlined both words. Then I took out my colored markers and drew a picture of a hamster. Ugh. It looked like a rock with eyes and a tail.

Wingnut waited. I told him that this looked like a tricky case. "Before we go any further," I said, "let me call my partner. Wait here."

I ran into the house and called Mila. Luckily she was home. "Meet me at the office," I told her. "We've got a case."

"Don't forget to put Rags inside," Mila reminded me. Mila was allergic to Rags. Anything with fur made her sneeze. So she tried to stay away from cats and dogs.

Mila lived around the corner, and we'd been friends since we were in diapers. Mila worked with me on all the big cases. I paid her fifty cents a day. Mila demanded equal pay for equal work. It was a lot of money — but she was worth every cent.

Mila was over in ten minutes. When Mila climbed up the ladder, she was humming "The Short Vowel Song." We learned it in Ms. Gleason's class last week.

Mila sang:

"Where is short a? Where is short a?
Here I am. Here I am.
I am in a hat rack,
Cracker Jacks, and fat cats;
'a' • 'a' • 'a,' 'a' • 'a' • 'a.'

"Where is short e? Where is short e?
Here I am. Here I am.
I am in a red bed,
jelly eggs, and jet sets;
'e' • 'e' • 'e,' 'e' • 'e' • 'e.' "

If Mila wasn't humming something, she was probably singing. I didn't mind. She had a pretty voice.

We all sat together on the floor of the office. I poured lemonade and told Mila about the missing hamster.

Mila was all business. "When did you see Hermie last?" she asked Wingnut.

"Yesterday morning," Wingnut sniffled. "He was in his cage with Sammy — that's my other hamster — happily gnawing on a piece of cardboard."

"How did you know he was happy?" I asked.

Wingnut shrugged. "I dunno. He just had a happy face, I guess."

"Show me," I said.

Wingnut was confused. "Does it matter?"

"Everything matters," I said. "A mystery is like a jigsaw puzzle. You can't put it together until you have all the pieces. Show me," I repeated. "What *exactly* did Hermie look like yesterday morning?"

Wingnut half closed his eyes. He puffed out his cheeks. He tightened his lips and poked out his two front teeth. I had to admit it: Wingnut looked like a happy hamster. Okay, a happy hamster . . . with really big ears.

"Thanks, Wingnut," I said. "You never know. That may be the missing piece we need to solve the mystery."

Mila twisted her long black hair and sighed. She asked Wingnut, "Did Hermie have any enemies?"

Wingnut thought for a moment. "No," he said. "Everybody loves Hermie, even Jake, and he's a teenager. Most teenagers don't like *anything*."

Jake, better known as "Jake the Snake," was Wingnut's big brother. He was fourteen years old and a little strange. People called him "Jake the Snake" because he loved snakes. I mean, this guy *really* loved snakes. He had snake books, snake T-shirts, snake posters. But most important of all, he had a pet snake. A rosy boa. It was pretty big. Sometimes Jake brought it outside, wrapped around his shoulders. It was long, smooth, and totally gross. To be honest, I didn't really like snakes. Not even from a distance.

Under the word "suspects" I wrote Jake.

In the beginning of a mystery, everyone is a suspect. And *anything* is possible.

"Think hard," I told Wingnut. "Would anyone, or anything, want to harm Hermie?"

Wingnut shrugged his shoulders. "Well, I guess an owl would love to get at Hermie. He'd make a nice meal."

"Disgusting," Mila said.

"Any other enemies?" I asked.

"A cat, maybe," Wingnut said. Then he thought some more. "A snake . . . a . . . "

Mila sat bolt upright. "Did you say *snake*?"

Wingnut got all worried looking. "You don't think . . . ?"

"Jake's snake is only a suspect," I told Wingnut. "We'll need to come over to your house and look for clues."

"Uh, okay. But it's almost dinnertime. I can't have friends over on school nights."

"Sure, Wingnut." I patted him on the back. "Maybe tomorrow after school. Don't worry, pal. We'll find Hermie."

Wingnut left us alone in the office. "What do you think?" I asked Mila.

"I think," she said, "that we need to do some research."

"About hamsters?" I asked.

"Yes," she said. "And about the eating habits of snakes."

Chapter Three

A Matter of Life and Death

On Monday morning I was standing in the rain under a bright pink umbrella. Don't laugh. I couldn't find my Batman umbrella, so I had to borrow my sister's pink one. It even had flowers on it. Yeesh. I'd rather get wet. Everybody knows tough guys hate pink.

But those are the breaks when you're the youngest. I've got three older brothers and an older sister. People say it's easy being the youngest in the family. Well, I've got news for you. People are wrong. If you're the youngest, you get bossed around. You never win a fight. Your brothers call you "Worm" and "Shorty." And your parents make you wear baggy hand-me-down clothes — and borrow your sister's pink umbrella.

At school, I sat in Ms. Gleason's class, Room 201. There were sixteen kids in our class, including Mila. It was an okay day — for a Monday. During science we learned about the seashore. And for social studies we studied Christopher Columbus.

Monday was also an art day. I got to draw whatever I wanted. It came out pretty good:

Mila and I got our chance right before lunch. It was time for desk work. Ms. Gleason was grading papers. We walked up to her desk.

"Ms. Gleason," I said.

Ms. Gleason looked up and smiled. "Yes, what can I do for you two?"

"We really, really need to learn about snakes and hamsters," I said.

Ms. Gleason put down her blue pencil. "This sounds serious."

"It is," Mila answered.

"Very serious," I whispered. "It's a matter of life and death."

Ms. Gleason put her hand over her mouth. Her eyes got wide. "Oh, goodness," she said.

"Can you help us?" I asked.

"Well, I'll certainly try," she replied.

Ms. Gleason looked at the wall clock. In her loud teacher voice she said, "Class, lunch is in two minutes. Please put away

your projects and line up along the wall." She looked at Charlie Maloney goofing around with Mike Radcliff. Ms. Gleason suddenly looked tired. She pushed her hair away from her face. "Without killing each other," she added.

Ms. Gleason turned back to us. "Well," she said, "I can think of a number of ways you can find out about hamsters and snakes. How about you?"

"I thought of one," I said. "Asking you."

Ms. Gleason smiled. "That's a start, Theodore. How about you, Mila?"

Mila answered, "Well, you could look in a book or . . . maybe talk to somebody who knows a lot."

"Yeah," I said. "Like an expert."

"Excellent," Ms. Gleason said. "One of you can go to the library, either here at school or in town. I'm sure a librarian could help you find many wonderful books.

You might also want to visit the computer room and try searching the Internet."

"My mom can probably take me to the library after school," Mila said.

I frowned. "What about me?"

"Well, Theodore," Ms. Gleason said, "it looks like it's your job to find an expert."

Oh, brother. I always get the dirty work.

Chapter Four

World of Reptiles

Our plan was set. After school, Mila went to the town library to read about snakes. It was my job to visit a local pet store, World of Reptiles. We decided to meet back at my house in an hour. There was only one problem. I needed a ride. Fortunately, my sixteen-year-old brother Billy had just gotten his driver's license. He always jumps at the chance of borrowing my mom's car.

Screech! Billy slammed on the brakes in

front of the pet store. He told me he'd pick me up in ten minutes.

"Make it fifteen," I said.

"You got it, Jigsaw."

Billy was my favorite brother. He was the only one who called me Jigsaw. My brothers Daniel and Nicholas were tied for second place. My sister, Hillary, came in last. I know it wasn't her fault, but I was still unhappy about the umbrella.

World of Reptiles was a dark, stuffy little store. There was one customer inside. He was a skinny man with a leather jacket and black boots.

Behind a counter sat a dark-haired woman. She smiled at me. She had a snake tattoo on her right arm. "Can I help you?" she asked.

"Just looking," I said.

Reptile tanks and cages lined the walls. This store had every kind of weird animal you could imagine. It had skinks, ferrets,

Gila monsters, box turtles, and talking parrots — even monkeys wearing diapers.

It also had snakes. Lots of snakes. Small skinny ones — and very, very big ones.

I stopped in front of the biggest cage. It was glass, about ten feet tall. Inside there was a yellow python thicker than my leg. It was curled up in a corner. It must have been thirty feet long.

"What does he eat?" I asked the lady.

She pointed to a large metal cage. I looked. It was filled with rabbits.

"He eats . . . bunnies?" I asked.

She nodded. I glanced at the cage again. Poor little fuzz balls.

Another customer went up to the counter. "I'll take six mice," he ordered.

After he left, I went up to the woman. "I didn't know people kept mice as pets," I said.

"Oh, no," she answered. "They aren't pets. The mice are food. Snake food."

I gulped. "Would a snake eat a hamster?"

She explained, "A snake would *love* to eat a hamster. But people buy the white mice instead. They're cheaper."

She came around the counter and led me to a cage. Inside were two rosy boas.

"Two weeks ago," she said, pointing at a tan snake with a reddish tip on its tail, "this slippery rascal got out. In the morning, I found him on top of the hamster cage."

"Did he eat the hamsters?" I asked.

She shook her head. "No, they were safe. The hamster lid was on tight." She pushed the wire roof. It didn't budge an inch.

"Can hamsters escape?" I asked.

"Sure," she said. "But only if the lid isn't on tight enough."

"But how do they get out?" I asked. "Can they climb glass walls like Spider-Man?"

"No," she said with a laugh. "They jump

and hang onto the edge. Actually, it's pretty amazing."

I thanked the nice woman and headed for the door. I'd seen enough snakes to last a lifetime.

Chapter Five

Bad News for Hermie

Back home, I sat down to eat a Popsicle. It made me feel better. This case was getting complicated. Things were not looking great for Hermie.

Plus I couldn't stop thinking about those rabbits. Somehow eating a mouse seemed okay. But a bunny — oh, brother. Just the thought of it made my stomach hurt.

Where was Mila? She should have been back by now. But if you put a book in front of Mila, she might never look up.

Suddenly I heard a voice.

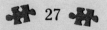

"Earth to Theodore, Earth to Theodore. Can you hear me?"

"MOM!" I cried. "I am NOT Theodore. I'm Jigsaw, Jigsaw Jones. And I'm working on a Very Important Case."

"I see," my mom answered. "Well, Mr. Jigsaw Jones," she said. "How about working on that room of yours? It's a disaster."

"Can't," I explained. "Things to do, mysteries to solve."

My mom put her hands on her hips. "Maybe I'm not being clear," she said. "I wasn't *asking*, I was *telling*. And now I'm *exclaiming*: Clean your room — now!"

So. She wanted to play tough.

I decided to hide out in my room for a while. Sorry, but cleaning a room was no job for the world's greatest second-grade detective. Somewhere out there a little hamster was depending on me. A little furry guy without a friend in the world. Maybe he was lost. Maybe he was stolen. Maybe he was lunch.

This was no time for putting away Legos.

I pulled out my detective journal and reviewed the facts of the case. I listed all the key words:

Hermie, Wingnut, Mystery, Missing, Boa, Python, World of Reptiles, and Jake.

I put the words in ABC order. It wasn't easy. Ms. Gleason said I needed

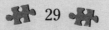

to practice my ABC order. My list looked like this:

Boa

Hermie

Jake

Missing

Mystery

Python

Wingnut

World of Reptiles

ABC order isn't that hard. Except I sometimes get mixed up with *M* and *N*. That's because whoever made up the alphabet got it all wrong. *N should* come first, then *M*. I mean, look at it this way. If you want to build an *M*, you start with an *N*. Then you just draw another line. But you can't draw an *M* without an *N* already waiting there. That's why I think the alphabet is inside out.

But try telling that to Ms. Gleason.

Bbbring! It was the doorbell.

"I'll get it!" I yelled. I raced to the door. It was Mila. She had three books in her arms.

And she looked worried.

Mila set the books down on our kitchen table. She wasn't humming. That meant bad news.

"I've been reading about snakes," she told me. "Look at what I found."

Mila opened a book to a picture of a snake. It had a mouse in its mouth. Correction: It had *half* a mouse in its mouth. The other half had already been swallowed.

"This snake is a rosy boa," Mila said. "The same kind of snake that Jake owns."

"Are they poisonous?" I asked.

"No, boas and pythons are in the constrictor family," Mila explained. She flipped through the pages of a book called *Killer Snakes*. Mila began reading out loud:

" 'Constrictors kill their prey by wrapping their bodies around them and squeezing. They squeeze until the victim stops breathing. They swallow their victims whole.' "

"Those constrictors remind me of my aunt Harriet," I told Mila. "My brother Billy calls her the Anaconda. When Aunt Harriet comes to visit, she can hug the life out of you."

I hugged myself and squeezed tight. Then I made all sorts of disgusting choking sounds. I fell on the floor, dead.

Mila didn't seem to notice.

We looked at more pictures. There was one of a snake swallowing an alligator. Then there was another picture of the same snake after it was done eating. It looked like a hat.

I took out my markers and drew a picture in my detective journal. It looked like this:

Mila said, "These snakes are giant pythons. They live in jungles in Africa and Asia. Jake's snake is a lot smaller."

I put my markers away. "Maybe Jake's snake is different. Maybe it doesn't eat mice. Maybe it just eats pizza. Or pretzels. Or something like that."

"Maybe," Mila said doubtfully. "But we still don't know if the snake had *opportunity*."

"Opportunity?" I asked.

"Yes, opportunity," Mila repeated. "We don't know if the snake could have gotten to Hermie's cage."

I stood up. "Then we'd better go," I said.

"Go?" she asked.

"Yes," I said. "Let's visit the scene of the crime."

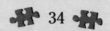

Chapter Six

Wingnut's Room

We had to ring the bell three times before Mrs. O'Brien answered the door. She had the handle of a big vacuum cleaner in her hand.

"Hello, Theodore. Hello, Mila." She smiled. "Have you been ringing long?" Mrs. O'Brien wiped her forehead with the back of her hand. "This new vacuum cleaner is so loud, I can't hear a thing."

Wingnut appeared at the door. We followed him into his room. It was spotless. "Sorry about the room," he apologized.

"My mom just bought a superpowerful vacuum cleaner. She's been cleaning for days. So don't leave anything lying around. She might suck it up!"

Yeesh. Wingnut's room gave me the creeps. It was clean, all right. *Too clean*. Everything was neat. Books were neatly on the shelves. Toys were neatly put away. Even the floor was neat. How can a guy live like that? It just wasn't normal.

Mila walked over to the hamster cage. It was on a low shelf, about knee-high.

One hamster lay curled up in the corner. "That's Sammy," Wingnut said. "He's sleeping. Hamsters mostly sleep all day. They like to run around at night."

"Ah-choo!" Mila sneezed.

"Bless you," I said.

The cage looked like a fish tank. Except it didn't have any water in it. And no fish. It

had a wire roof. Mila poked at it. The roof moved a little, but not much. I doubted that a hamster could get through a hole that small.

"Do you always keep the lid on?" I asked.

"Yes," Wingnut said. "I'm really careful about it. One night, after cleaning the cage, I forgot to put it back on. Hermie escaped. We didn't find him for two whole days."

Mila sneezed . . . and sneezed again.

I got tired of saying "Bless you" all the time. But like my dad says, "Having manners is a full-time job." Even if you have to say the same thing — over and over and over again.

I tried to imagine what it would be like to eat a hamster. Mila and Wingnut watched as I slithered on the ground. I flicked my tongue into the air. I looked at Sammy in the cage. Yuck! I was glad that I wasn't a snake. I'd rather eat pizza.

"Where is the snake?" Mila asked. She

looked at me crawling on the floor. "The real one," she added.

"Across the hall," Wingnut answered. "In Jake's room."

"Can we see it?" she asked.

"Sure. I don't think Jake's home," Wingnut said.

"I don't know," I said. "Teenagers don't like people in their rooms."

"Aw, come on," Wingnut said. "It's no big deal."

Jake's door had a sign on it. It said:

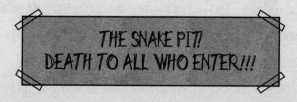

THE SNAKE PIT!
DEATH TO ALL WHO ENTER!!!

Wingnut knocked. No one answered. Wingnut slowly pushed open the door.

We stepped inside. It was dark. And creepy. And it smelled like snake.

That's when Mila screamed.

Chapter Seven

Enter the Snake Pit

"EEEECK!"

I must have jumped about fifty million feet. Mila pointed at a stereo speaker. There it was — the rosy boa. Curled up in a ball. It looked calm and peaceful. The problem was, it wasn't in a cage. I felt a little wiggle in my stomach.

Wingnut said, "Don't be afraid. Jake lets him out of the cage all the time."

I stood behind Mila.

"He's harmless," Wingnut said. "Jake says that snakes are the most misunderstood creatures in the animal kingdom."

Wingnut petted the snake's smooth skin. "See? Snakes don't like to bother anybody."

"Tell that to a mouse," Mila muttered.

"Or a bunny," I added.

I looked around. Jake sure had a weird room. The lightbulbs were black. They gave off a strange light that made Mila's white shirt glow. He had posters all over the walls. Mostly basketball stars, snakes, and a goofy one of a bunch of dogs playing cards. Go figure.

Just then, the door flew open. It was Jake — and he looked mad. "What are you pip-squeaks doing in my room?" he roared. "Didn't you read the sign?"

I felt another wiggle in my stomach.

Wingnut stepped forward. "Sorry, Jake. It was an emergency." He pointed at me. "Jigsaw is a detective. He's trying to help me find Hermie."

Jake looked at me. "A pip-squeak detective, eh? Well, try again, Sherlock. You can bet Hermie's not in here. Or else Goliath would have gotten him."

Goliath, I guessed, was Jake's boa.

"Actually," I said, "I was wondering if Goliath had opportunity."

"Opportunity?" Jake asked.

"Yes," I said. "Could it have slithered into Wingnut's room?"

Jake shook his head. "No way, no how. Goliath doesn't leave this room unless I take him."

"Are you positive?" Mila asked.

"Sure I am," Jake said. "Besides, if he got out, I would have known about it. Or my mom would have seen him. She's been vacuuming everything in sight for days."

Jake picked up the snake. He brought him to Mila. "Here," Jake said, "touch him."

Mila touched Goliath. "He's not slimy at all," she said.

"How about you?" Jake said, bringing the snake to me.

"Er, no thanks," I said.

Jake brought the snake closer to my face. "Come on," he said.

Jake wasn't being very nice. After all, I didn't like snakes. My stomach jiggled and wiggled. I suddenly felt dizzy. Like I'd just eaten three hot dogs — and gone on a roller coaster about eight times in a row.

Like I was going to get sick or something.

And I did.

Right on Jake's Air Jordans.

Chapter Eight

Person, Place, or Thing

There was a knock on my bedroom door.

"I'm not here," I moaned.

My brother Billy walked in. "I heard about what happened. How are you feeling, tough guy?" he asked.

"Rotten," I said.

Billy put down a plate of buttered toast and a cup of honey tea on my night table. "Mom said you should try to eat something," he said.

"I'm never going to eat again," I said.

Billy sat on the edge of my bed. "Don't

take it so hard, Jigsaw. Everybody throws up."

"Not on somebody's sneakers," I said.

Billy smiled. "I wish I had been there to see Jake's face. He must have freaked."

I sort of laughed, too. It *was* pretty funny.

"How's the case going?" Billy asked.

"Rotten," I said. "There's no way Jake's boa could have done it. I'm ready to give up."

Billy put his hand on my shoulder. "You'll solve the mystery," he said. "Keep working at it."

After the toast and tea, my stomach felt a little better. But my heart still felt lousy. I was worried about Hermie. Where was he? Could someone have stolen him? Was he still alive?

I figured that working on a jigsaw puzzle might make me feel better. I had a new one that I hadn't opened yet. It was called "Monsters of Hollywood." I laid all the pieces on the floor. You can't start a puzzle until you've looked at every piece.

Jigsaws were like mysteries. . . .

"That's it!" I said. I grabbed my detective journal. Maybe I had missed a clue. I needed to look at all the pieces again.

In school we were learning about the parts of speech. I decided to do the same thing with the facts of the case. On top of one page, I wrote the word PERSON. On the next page, I wrote **PLACE**. On the one after that, I wrote **THING**.

Then I thought about everything that had to do with the case. And I mean *everything*.

My final lists looked like this:

PERSON	PLACE	THING
Wingnut	World of Reptiles	Hermie
Jake	My office	Sammy
Pet store owner	Wingnut's room	Goliath (Jake's snake)
Jigsaw (ME!)	Library	Vacuum cleaner
Mila	Jake's room	Vomit
Wingnut's mom	School (Room 201!)	Hamster cage
Ms. Gleason		

It was mostly pretty easy. I wasn't so sure about the **THING** column. I mean, I knew Hermie wasn't a person or a place. But he seemed like *more* than just a **THING**.

Looking at all the facts seemed to help. I thought about Wingnut . . . and Hermie . . .

and Jake . . . and World of Reptiles. Something was bothering me.

I closed my eyes and tried to remember my visit to the store.

I remembered the man buying the mice. I remembered the poor bunnies, the nice lady's tattoo, the hamster cage. Then it hit me. *KLUNK!* Like a baseball bat smashed on my head.

When the lady pushed the hamster roof, it didn't budge. But in Wingnut's room, the hamster roof was loose. Not very loose. Just a little.

Maybe that was enough.

Maybe Hermie had escaped after all!

He might still be alive. Then I began to worry. How long could a hamster survive without food?

I switched off the light and went back to bed. School tomorrow. It was going to be another busy day.

Chapter Nine
The Phony Clue

"Okay, class," Ms. Gleason said. "It's organization time. You know your jobs."

At last the school day was almost over. Now all we had to do was get ready for tomorrow. We had to clean up, sharpen our pencils, and get our coats. Plus some kids had special jobs at the end of the day. There were Board Cleaners and Book Checkers. Chair Putter-Uppers and Closet Neateners and Homework Checkers. The best job was Zookeeper. But our gerbil died a few weeks ago. So now we were the only second-grade class in the whole school without a pet. We didn't need a Zookeeper anymore.

I had a free day. So I neatened up my desk superfast.

I raised my hand. "Ms. Gleason," I said.

Ms. Gleason came over to my desk. "Thank you for raising your hand, Theodore," Ms. Gleason said. "And by the way," she whispered, "how's that matter of life and death coming along?"

"Not so great," I said. "I threw up on Jake O'Brien's sneakers yesterday."

"Oh," Ms. Gleason answered. "That's not fun." She moved back a step.

"And I have another problem." I told her that I needed to find a phone number.

"That's not a problem," she said.

"It is," I answered, "if you don't know how."

Ms. Gleason walked to her desk and

pulled out a big, fat phone book. She explained, "Phone books are in two parts, Theodore. The first part is called the white pages. It lists the phone numbers of all the people who live in our area." She flipped through the book. "This other section is called the yellow pages. See? The pages are yellow. It lists the phone numbers for all the businesses."

"Super," I said. "Could you tell me the phone number for World of Reptiles?"

Ms. Gleason smiled. "No," she said. "You'll have to look it up yourself." She handed me the book. "Everything is in alphabetical order," she said. "By category."

"Category?" I asked. This wasn't turning out so hot.

"Yes. What *kind* of business is World of Reptiles? Is it a restaurant? Do they serve lizard stew?" Ms. Gleason laughed at her joke.

I didn't laugh. I told Ms. Gleason that it was the name of the pet store.

"Then you can start by looking under *P*, for pets."

Oh, brother. Teachers. You try to get a simple answer and all you get is more work.

By the time I found the phone number, it was nearly time to go. I put on my jacket and lined up for the bell. I found a note inside my pocket. It was in code:

20–8–9–19*9–19*I*6–1–11–5*3–12–21–5.

I knew the note was from Mila. She was always testing my brainpower. I'd seen a code like this before. It was called a substitution code. All you had to do was write out the alphabet. Then you had to write the numbers one to twenty-six underneath each letter. They worked together in pairs. Each number in Mila's code stood for a letter. I solved it on the bus.

Then I scribbled a quick message to Mila. I figured that I'd put it on her desk tomorrow. It looked like this:

Chapter Ten

Another Fine Mess

I called World of Reptiles right after school. The pet store owner was very nice. She told me everything I needed to know. Then I raced over to Wingnut's house. There wasn't any time to lose.

"Is your mom home?" I asked Wingnut.

"Nope," Wingnut said. "She went food shopping."

"Good," I said. "Jake?"

"He's in his room." Loud music throbbed from behind Jake's door.

I hesitated. "Do you think it's safe?"

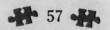

Wingnut nodded. "Jake said he never wants to be in the same room with you again."

"Fine with me," I said. "We have to work fast. I think I know where Hermie is."

Wingnut was thrilled — until I told him where. "I don't know, Jigsaw," he said. "My mom might get really mad. It's a brand-new vacuum cleaner."

I looked at him. "Do you want to find Hermie or not?"

Wingnut was still nervous. But he brought the vacuum cleaner into the living room anyway.

The clues had been in front of me all the time. The new vacuum cleaner . . . the superclean bedroom . . . the wobbly hamster lid.

I explained it again to Wingnut. "Listen, pal. It all makes sense." I leaned closer to him and whispered in his ear. "I just talked on the phone with the lady from World of

Reptiles. She told me that hamsters are really good squeezers. They can squeeze through the teeniest, tiniest holes. That lid of yours wasn't on tight enough," I said. "That's how Hermie escaped."

Wingnut was nervous. "But what does my mom's vacuum cleaner have to do with it?"

"Think, Wingnut. Jake said that your mom's been vacuuming everything in sight. There isn't a speck of dust in your room. That was a clue. I bet that your mom vacuumed in there — around the same time Hermie escaped."

Wingnut looked at the vacuum cleaner. "You don't think . . . ?"

I nodded. "Hermie's in there."

Opening up the vacuum cleaner wasn't easy. There were a few weird latches that I didn't understand. I tried prying it open with a screwdriver — but that didn't work.

"Have you got a hammer?" I asked.

A few good whacks did the job. Unfortunately, it did a little too good of a job. Part of the vacuum cleaner shattered, sending pieces of plastic flying through the air.

"Jigsaw!" Wingnut exclaimed. "Be careful!"

I looked at Wingnut. It seemed like he might start crying again. "Don't worry, pal," I said. "With a little tape, it will be as good as new."

I emptied the vacuum bag on the carpet. Dust flew everywhere. "We'll clean up this mess later," I said. "Let's start looking for Hermie."

We were finished in ten minutes. We found two toys from Wingnut's Star Wars collection — Chewbacca and R2-D2. We found six rubber bands and a paper clip. We found a purple crayon and half of a Ken Griffey baseball card. We even found hamster hair.

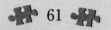

But we didn't find Hermie.

Unfortunately, Mrs. O'Brien found us — sitting on the rug, surrounded by dirt and dust and broken plastic. The vacuum cleaner was in pieces.

I can't really blame her for screaming.

Chapter Eleven
The Ah-choo Clue

We heard Mila coming even before she knocked. She was singing again:

"Where is short i? Where is short i?
Here I am. Here I am.
I am in a big fig,
Silly Rick, and pig wig;
'i' • 'i' • 'i,' 'i' • 'i' • 'i.'

"Where is short o? Where is short o?
Here I am. Here I am.
I am in a hot pot,

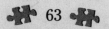

Rocky top, and stop clock;
'o' • 'o' • 'o,' 'o' • 'o' • 'o.' "

"Hey, guys." She saw our sad faces. "What's wrong?"

"I'm in big trouble," Wingnut said. "And it's all his fault."

"I said I was sorry about a million times already," I complained.

Mila looked around. "Hey, where's your hamster cage?"

"I'm keeping Sammy in my parents' room," Wingnut said. "I think he's safer there."

I didn't listen to them. I was trying to think. The snake didn't get Hermie. The vacuum cleaner didn't get Hermie. Where could he be?

Mila leaned against the closet door and sneezed. "Ah-choo!" Then she sneezed again.

I was in a rotten mood. "Mila," I snapped.

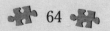

"Could you *please* stop sneezing? I'm trying to think."

Mila folded her arms. "I can't help it, Jigsaw. You know I'm allergic to fur. I always sneeze if I get too close to it."

"But there isn't any fur in my room," Wingnut said. "Hermie is gone and so is Sammy."

Mila sneezed again. "Well," she sniffled, "something is making me sneeze."

Mila and I looked at each other. We shouted at once: "HERMIE!"

The search was on!

Wingnut looked under the bed. I took the closet. Mila searched through the toy chest.

We didn't find a thing.

We were about to give up when I had an idea. A crazy idea. A wonderful, fantastic, crazy idea.

"Have you guys ever heard of metal detectors?" I asked.

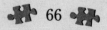

Mila spoke up. "Sure, people use them to find old coins and stuff like that. If the detector comes near metal, it beeps."

"That's right," I said.

Mila shrugged. "So?"

"So . . . we've got a hamster detector right here. But instead of beeping, it sneezes," I answered. "It's you, Mila!"

It was worth a try. Mila slowly walked around the room. She didn't sneeze until she got near the closet. "Ah-choo!"

"Stop!" I yelled.

Mila sneezed again. She got down on her hands and knees. Then she really started sneezing like crazy.

Wingnut and I got down next to her. All three of us crawled into the closet. Mila put her nose next to a poster tube that was lying on the floor. She sneezed on it. Three times.

I looked inside.

I couldn't believe my eyes.

I patted Wingnut on the back. "Guess what, pal. We've found Hermie. But there's just one thing you should know," I said. "Hermie is a . . . SHE!"

Wingnut looked into the tube. He saw Hermie nestled inside the tube . . . feeding baby hamsters!

Wingnut was confused. "If Hermie is a she . . . " he said.

"Then Sammy is a daddy!" Mila added.

We left Wingnut alone in his room. He was happily cooing into the cardboard tube.

"Happy birthday, little guys," he gently whispered.

Chapter Twelve

Student of the Week!

A week later, I walked into World of Reptiles. I was singing a new song that I'd just made up:

"Where is Herm-ie? Where is Herm-ie?
Here I am. Here I am.
I am in a new cage,
loving all my babies.
Her–er–me. Her–er–me."

"Hello again," said the nice lady. "You seem happy today."

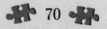
70

"Oh, I am," I said. "I'm very happy." I told her about the hamster babies. And I thanked her for all the help.

"So what brings you here?" she asked.

"Supplies," I said. "My teacher and I are cooking up a surprise for the whole class."

* * *

The school bell rang. But I waited outside the classroom door. It was part of the secret plan. I could hear Ms. Gleason talking to the class.

"Settle down, boys and girls," said Ms. Gleason. "As you know, Black Fang the gerbil died recently. It was a sad time for us all. But today Theodore and I have a special surprise for you."

Ms. Gleason opened the door. "Come in, Theodore."

I walked in, holding the surprise in my arms. No one could tell what I had because it was hidden under a sheet. I smiled at Mila — she was the only person who knew about the secret.

"Children," Ms. Gleason said, "I'd like you to meet our new class members — ta-da!" She pulled off the sheet.

I was holding a brand-new hamster cage. Inside, there were two baby hamsters — gifts from Wingnut O'Brien.

Everyone cheered and hooted.

"Theodore, please put our new friends on the back shelf."

Everyone watched as I walked to the back of the room.

Ms. Gleason said, "Class, I think Theodore deserves a big round of applause. Because it was all his idea."

The kids cheered again, even louder than before. I was proud. And so was Mila. It couldn't have happened without her help. Sure, she was still allergic to hamsters. But Mila said it wasn't a problem if she didn't

get too close to them. The only bad thing was, Mila could never be Zookeeper.

"One last thing," Ms. Gleason said. "I've decided to name Theodore Student of the Week."

She handed me a piece of paper with beautiful squiggly lines all around it. Ms. Gleason called it a certificate.

When I sat down at the table, everyone at my table wanted to look at it. Mila read it out loud:

STUDENT of the WEEK

Theodore Jones has been named Student of the Week because _he gave Room 201 two pet hamsters_. Thanks for helping to make our classroom a nicer place. I am so proud of you!

CONGRATULATIONS!
Ms. Gleason
Room 201

Mila put down the certificate and smiled.

I looked around. Everybody was smiling. Even Ms. Gleason.

Good old Wingnut, I thought. It was nice of him to give us those hamsters.

But now the case was closed. I needed a new mystery to solve. Somehow I knew there would be one. There always was.

Like I said before, I make problems go away. And there are always problems — missing cupcakes, stolen baseball mitts, lost hamsters . . .

There will always be a need for me: Jigsaw Jones, Private Eye.